Who Am I?

Written and illustrated by
Jeffrey Turner

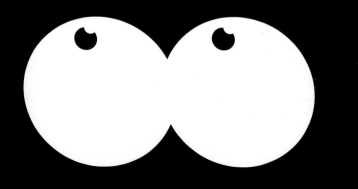

For Mark and Evan

ALADDIN / An imprint of Simon & Schuster Children's Publishing Division / 1230 Avenue of the Americas, New York, New York 10020 / First Aladdin hardcover edition October 2017 / Copyright © 2017 by Jeffrey Turner / All rights reserved, including the right of reproduction in whole or in part in any form. / ALADDIN and related logo are registered trademarks of Simon & Schuster, Inc. / For information about special discounts for bulk purchases, please contact Simon & Schuster Special Sales at 1-866-506-1949 or business@simonandschuster.com. / The Simon & Schuster Speakers Bureau can bring authors to your live event. For more information or to book an event contact the Simon & Schuster Speakers Bureau at 1-866-248-3049 or visit our website at www.simonspeakers.com. / Book designed by Nina Simoneaux / The illustrations for this book were rendered digitally. / The text of this book was set in Nanami HM Book. / Manufactured in China 0817 SCP / 2 4 6 8 10 9 7 5 3 1 / Library of Congress Control Number 2017931486 / ISBN 978-1-4814-5304-2 (hc) / ISBN 978-1-4814-5305-9 (eBook)

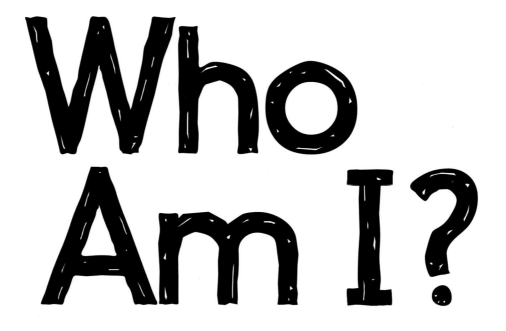

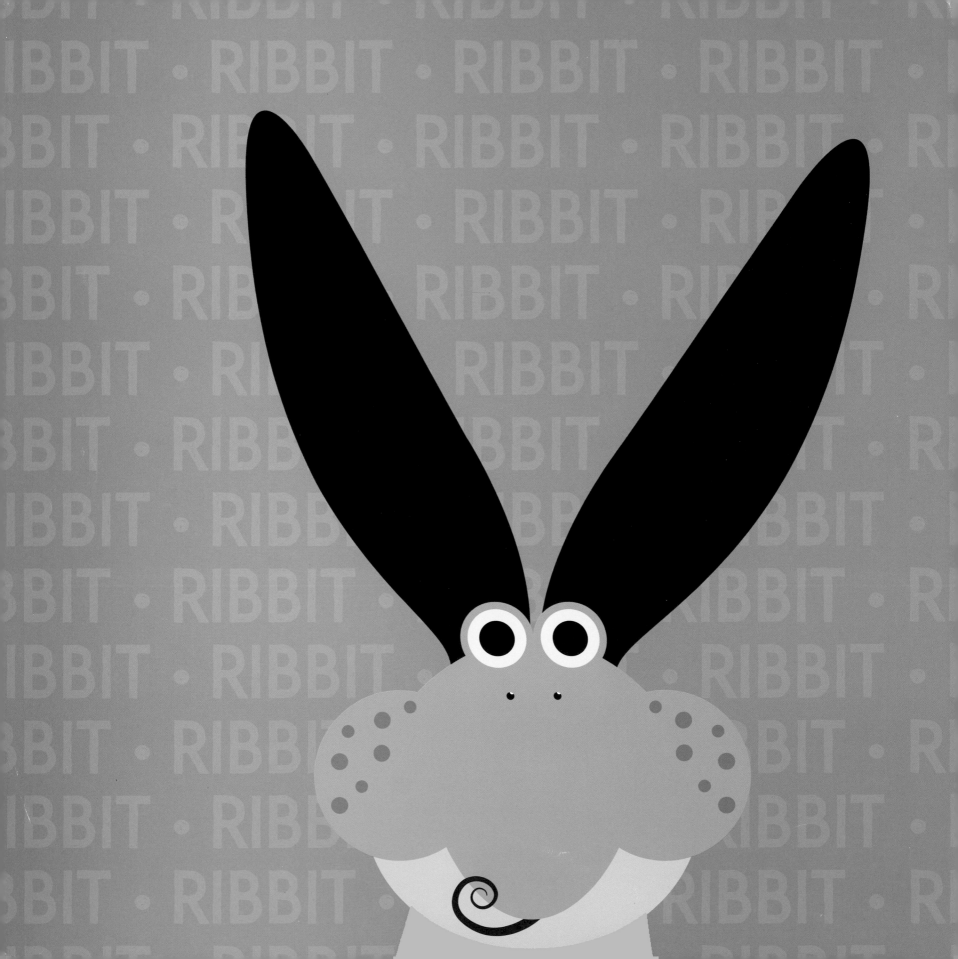

I am a frog.

RIBBIT!

You are not a frog.
You are a rabbit!

I am a rooster.
COCK-A-DOODLE-DOO!

You are not a rooster
or a frog.
You are a rabbit!

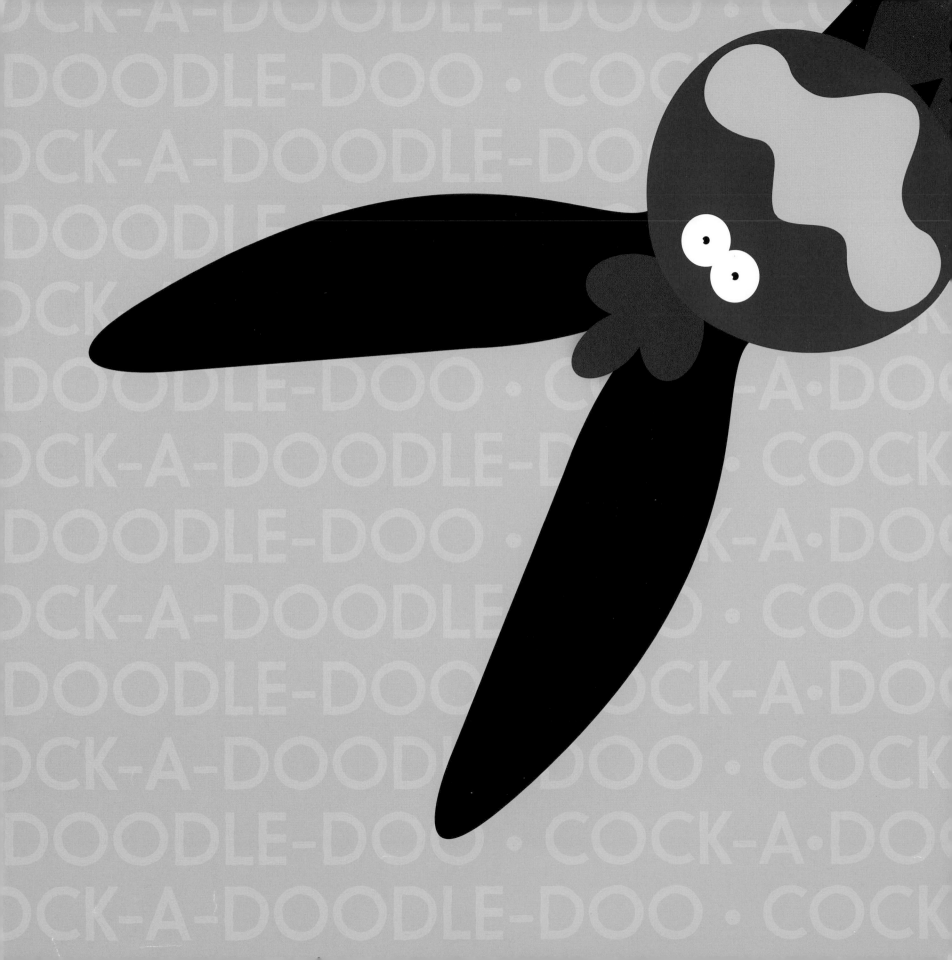

I am a tiger.
GRRRRRR!

You are not a tiger,
a rooster, or a frog.
You are a rabbit!

I am a mouse.
SQUEAK!

You are not a mouse, a tiger, a rooster, or a frog.
You are a rabbit!

SQUEAK • SQUEAK
SQUEAK • SQUEAK • SQUEAK
SQUEAK • SQUEAK
SQUEAK • SQUEAK
SQUEAK • SQUEAK
SQUEAK
SQUEAK
SQUEAK • SQUEAK
SQUEAK
SQUEAK
SQUEAK • SQUEAK
SQUEAK
SQUEAK • SQUEAK

I am an owl.
HOOT!

You are not an owl,
a mouse, a tiger,
a rooster, or a frog.
You are a rabbit!

I am a sheep.
BAA!

You are not a sheep,
an owl, a mouse, a tiger,
a rooster, or a frog.
You are a rabbit!

I am a monkey.
OOK-OOK!

You are not a monkey,
a sheep, an owl, a mouse,
a tiger, a rooster, or a frog.
You are a rabbit!

I am a pig.

OINK!

You are not a pig, a monkey, a sheep, an owl, a mouse, a tiger, a rooster, or a frog. You are a rabbit!

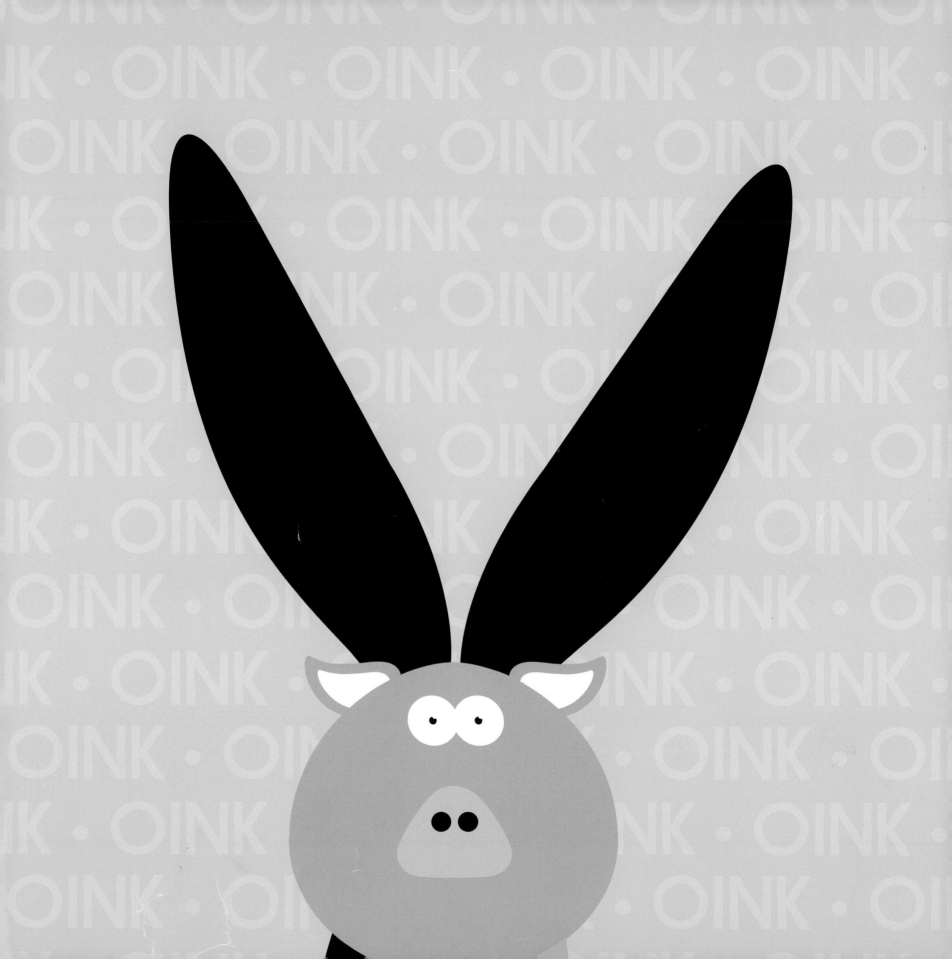

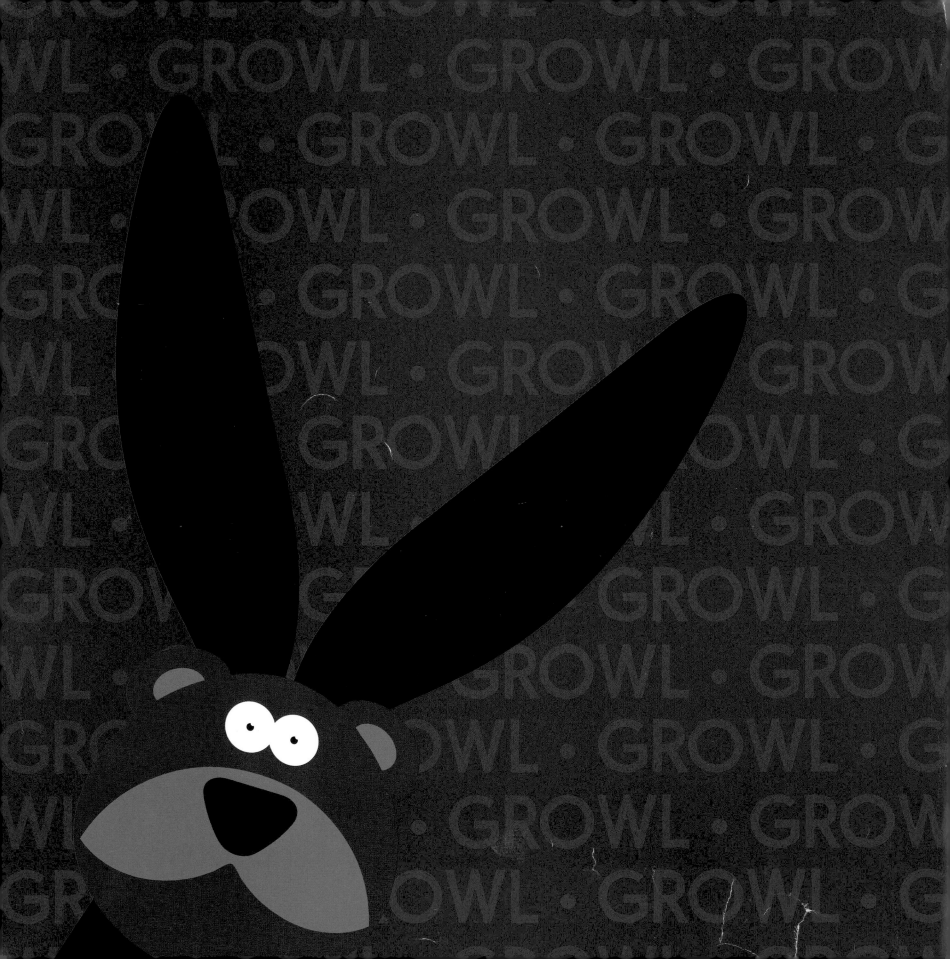

I am a bear.
GROWL!

You are not a bear, a
pig, a monkey, a sheep,
an owl, a mouse, a tiger,
a rooster, or a frog.
You are a rabbit!

I am a fox.
OW-OW-OW!

You are not a fox, a bear, a pig, a monkey, a sheep, an owl, a mouse, a tiger, a rooster, or a frog.
You are a rabbit!

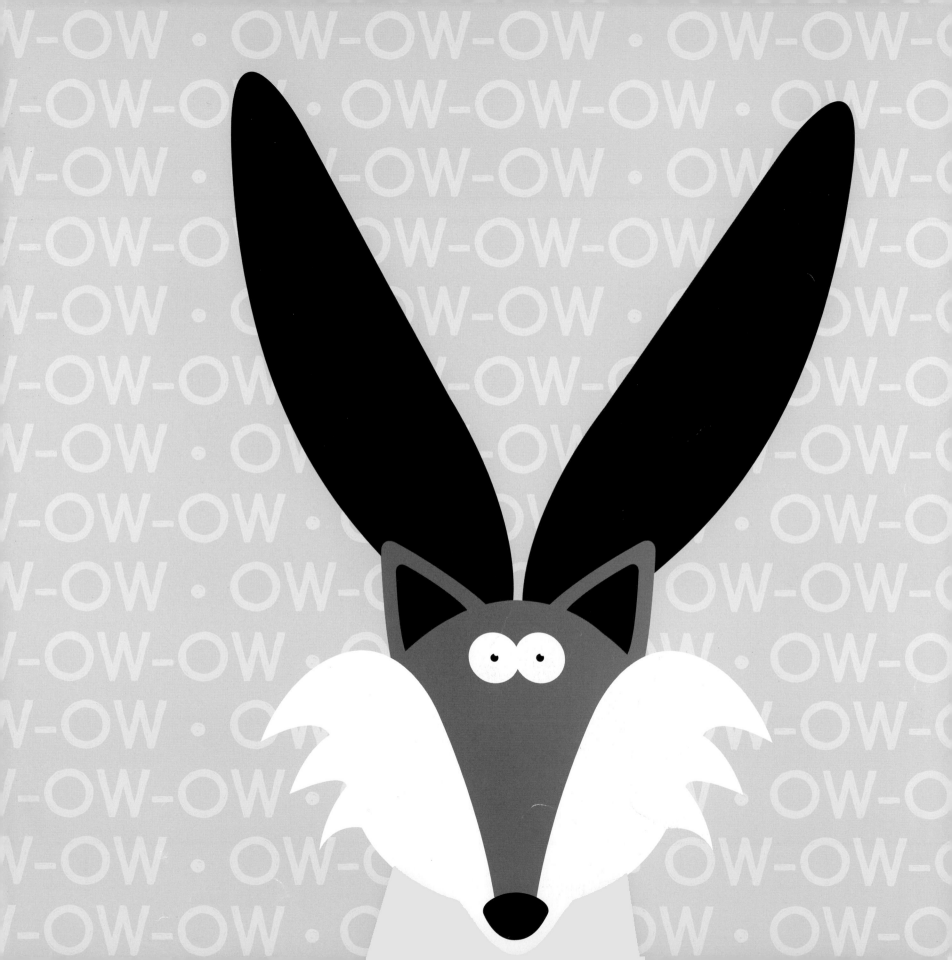

I am a peacock.
MAY-AWE!

You are not a peacock, a fox,
a bear, a pig, a monkey, a
sheep, an owl, a mouse, a tiger,
a rooster, or a frog.
You are a rabbit!

A rabbit?

Yes, a rabbit!

But I love to oink.
I love to squeak.
I love to cock-a-doodle-doo.

By the way, what are you?

A dog?

Yes. A dog!

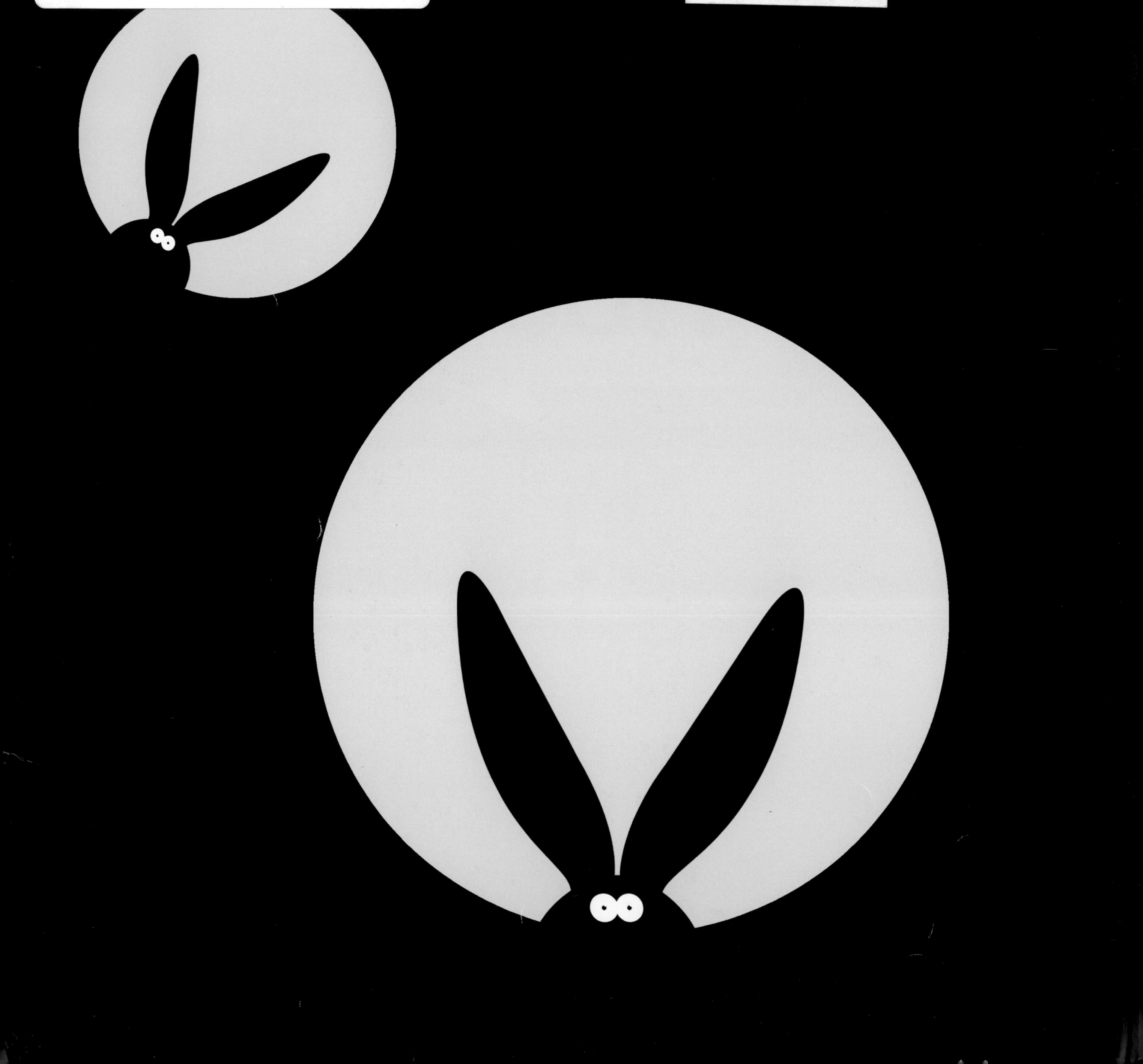